and Information

This book belongs to:

....

....

For Serena, the original Little Bear and Mum,
for her love and inspiration ~ SQ

Here's to a wonderful and colourful year of spending
time in the company of good friends and family ~ CP

Editor: Alexandra Koken
Designer: Verity Clark

Copyright © QED Publishing 2013

First published in the UK in 2013 by QED Publishing
A Quarto Group company, 230 City Road, London EC1V 2TT

www.qed-publishing.co.uk

A catalogue record for this book is available from the British Library.

ISBN 978 1 78171 129 3

Printed in China

Little Bear and the Butterflies

Susan Quinn and Caroline Pedler

QED Publishing

Little Bear was trying to catch a butterfly.

"When I was little, chasing
butterflies in Bluebell
Meadow was my favourite
game," said Mummy Bear.

Little Bear yawned.
"Can I go to Bluebell Meadow?"

"Later," said Mummy Bear.
"But now it's time for your nap."

Little Bear was almost asleep
when something tickled her nose.

It was a butterfly!

Little Bear stood up
and stretched.

She followed the
butterfly along the riverbank
and into the wood.

Little Bear tripped over a
tree root and landed on
her bottom.

"Watch out!"
shouted Rabbit.

"I was following a butterfly to Bluebell Meadow," Little Bear said. "But now the butterfly has gone."

"I'd like to go to Bluebell Meadow too," said Rabbit. "Let's see if Mouse knows the way."

"Oh hello," said Mouse. "I'm just piling up leaves to bounce on. Would you like to help me?"

"We'd love to," said Little Bear. Soon there was a mountain of leaves higher than Mouse and Rabbit.

"This is fun!"
they squealed,
bouncing up
and down.

"Now we need to find Bluebell Meadow,"
Little Bear explained to Mouse.

"Let's ask Owl," said Mouse.
"He knows everything."

So Little Bear
climbed Owl's tree . . .

"I'm trying to sleep!"
grumbled Owl.

"Sorry," said Little Bear, "but
do you know the way to
Bluebell Meadow?"

"Just follow the
butterflies," Owl said.

Little Bear, Rabbit and Mouse sat on
a rock and waited for butterflies.

And waited.

"I don't think we'll ever find Bluebell
Meadow," Little Bear said sadly.

Then something fluttered

past her nose.

"A butterfly!" squeaked Mouse.
"Quick!" cried Little Bear, jumping to her feet.

Little Bear, Rabbit and Mouse
followed the butterfly through
the wood.

They followed it up the hill,
and down the other side.

And when they got to
the top of the next hill, they saw . . .

...a meadow of bluebells and

butterflies dancing in the sunlight.

"We found Bluebell Meadow!"
shouted Little Bear.

They played **hide and seek**
among the bluebells.

They played **peek-a-boo,**
and made daisy chains.

But mostly they chased the butterflies.

"This is the best day ever!" Rabbit said flopping on the grass.

"I could stay here forever," said Little Bear sleepily.

"Wake up! It's teatime,"
said Mummy Bear.
Little Bear opened her eyes.

"But I've been to Bluebell Meadow
with Rabbit and Mouse," she said.

"It was just a dream," said Mummy Bear.
"It seemed so real!" said Little Bear.
"Good dreams are like that," Mummy Bear
said, giving her a great big bear hug.

Next steps

Show the children the cover again. What did the children think the book would be about before they heard the story? How is the story different?

Why do the children think Little Bear and Rabbit helped Mouse to make his pile of leaves? Ask the children to talk about an occasion when they helped one of their friends. What did they do? How did it make them feel?

Why do the children think Owl was grumpy? Ask the children why Owl was trying to sleep in the middle of the afternoon. Ask them how they feel if they are woken up suddenly.

Ask the children to talk about their best day ever. What made it so special?

Ask the children to draw and cut out paper butterflies. Perhaps arrange them into sizes and colours and ask the children to count them.

Look at the picture of Little Bear on the last page. Ask the children whether they can see a difference between Little Bear here and in the first picture in the book. Can they suggest why she is wearing a daisy chain around her neck in the last picture?

Ask the children if they think Little Bear's trip to Bluebell Meadow was a dream or a magical adventure. If it was magic, do the children think Mummy Bear might be magical? Or the butterfly?